Adventures

MAURICIO

#4

SHOULD I SAY YES... TO NICK NOPE?

NEW YORK

Monica

Monica is a sweet, happy, buck-toothed, teenage girl. When she was younger, she was known for being intolerant of disrespect and always stood up for her friends. That is, unless Jimmy-Five and Smudge would cause her trouble, then Monica would bash them with her favorite plush blue bunny, Samson! Still, occasionally, she does her classic bunny bashings as a teen, but has chilled out when it comes to Jimmy-Five, who has been catching her attention a lot more lately. Monica is the leader of the gang because of her honest and charisma-tic—and powerful—personality.

J-Five

Jimmy-Five, or J-Five, has always been picked on for his speech impediment. He used to lisp, which caused him to switch letters around, such as r's for w's, when he would speak. He has grown out of that as a teen, unless he's nervous, which typically happens around a certain girl. He also was picked on because of the five strands of hair he had on his head, which have all sort of filled out as a teen. Still, J-Five is sometimes made fun of for his hair, but he doesn't let it get to him as much anymore! When J-Five was young, he would often try to steal Monica's blue bunny from her and attempt to take over as leader of the gang with his questionable schemes. J-Five is no longer focused on being head of the gang as much as he's focused on being close with his friends, and closer to one friend in particular...

Smudge

Smudge has never liked water and prefers his messy and dirty lifestyle over showers, rain, swimming, or even drinking water any day, but he's warmed up to taking showers as a teen… sort of. He cleans up sometimes mainly because the opinion of girls has started to matter to him, unlike when he was a kid. Smudge loves sports, especially skateboarding and soccer because of how radical they are. He also loves comics, and shares this love with his best friend, J-Five! Smudge is kind of the "handyman" of the gang, always helping his friends in times of need but typically also messing everything up.

Maggy

Maggy is Monica's best friend, always having her back and being there for her in good times and bad. Maggy is also a huge lover of cats. Maggy has always had a voracious appetite, mostly eating watermelons but never discriminating against any other food put in front of her. Maggy is more conscious of what she eats now… perhaps a little too much. She is virtually obsessed with proper nutrition, sports, and exercise instead of eating anything she sees.

#4 "Should I Say Yes...to Nick Nope?"

Characters, Story, and Illustration created by MAURICIO DE SOUSA
ZAZO AGUIAR and WELLINGTON DIAS—Cover Artists
PETRA LEÃO—Script
MARCELO CASSARO—Layout
DENIS Y. OYAFUSO, JOSÉ APARECIDO CAVALCANTE, LINO PAES, and ROBERTO M. PEREIRA—Pencils
CRISTINA H. ANDO, FÁBIO ASADA, JAIME PODAVIN, ROSANA G. VALIM, TATIANA M. SANTOS, VIVIANE YAMABUCHI, WELLINGTON DIAS, and ZAZO AGUIAR—Inks
CARLOS KINA—Original Lettering
A. MAURICIO SOUSA NETO, ANTÔNIO R. F. GUEDES—Finishes
JAE HYUNG WOO, CAMILA FERNANDES, FÁBIO ASADA, KAIO RENATO BRUDER,MARCELO KINA, and MARIA JÚLIA S. BELLUCCI—Colorists
MARIA DE FÁTIMA A. CLARO, MARIA APARECIDA RABELLO, and JAE HYUNG WOO—Art Coordination
MAURICIO DE SOUSA, MARINA TAKEDA E SOUSA, and SANDRO ANTONIO DA SILVA—Script Supervisors
ALICE K. TAKEDA—Executive Director
SIDNEY GUSMAN—Editorial Planner
WAGNER BONILLA—Art Director
ÍVANA MELLO, SOLANGE M. LEMES—Original editors
Special thanks to LOURDES GALIANO, GRACIELE PEREIRA, RODRIGO PAIVA, TATIANE COMLOSI, MARINA TAKEDA E SOUSA, MÔNICA SOUSA, and MAURICO DE SOUSA

Originally published as Turma da Mônica Jovem #29 by Panini Comics.

www.turmadamonica.com.br

BRYAN SENKA—Letterer
JEFF WHITMAN—Editor, Translator
IZZY BOYCE-BLANCHARD—Editorial Intern
JIM SALICRUP
Editor-in-Chief

Charmz is an imprint of Papercutz.

ISBN: 978-1-5458-0339-4

Printed in the USA
December 2019

Charmz books may be purchased for business or promotional use.
For information on bulk purchases please contact Macmillan Corporate and Premium Sales Department at
(800) 221-7945 x5442

Distributed by Macmillan
First Charmz Printing

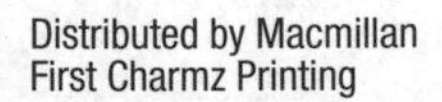

MAURICIO
EXCUSE ME, GOOD AFTERNOON...

M-MAY I COME IN?
WHAT'S UP WITH YOU, MONICA?

NO NEED TO BE SO FORMAL, HONEY.
LIKE YOU'VE NEVER BEEN OVER BEFORE.

I KNOW EXACTLY WHO YOU CAME TO SEE.
HE'S IN HIS ROOM. I'LL GO GET HIM--
NO! HEE-HEE... IF YOU DON'T MIND...

...COULD I GO UP TO HIS ROOM?
I NEED TO TALK TO HIM ABOUT SOMETHING... IMPORTANT.

AH! I THINK I UNDERSTAND...
SURE! GO AHEAD UP.

I ALWAYS SAY... MY SON CAN BE A DIFFICULT PERSON...

...BUT HE LIKES HAVING YOU AROUND, MONICA.

HE... DOES?
THEN... WHY AM I SO **NERVOUS?**

HELLO?! IT'S ME!
I HOPE I'M NOT INTERRUPTING YOU OR ANYTHING...

HONESTLY... YOU **ARE** INTERRUPTING ME.

OH! I-I'M S-SO SORRY...
⁼PSH!⁼ NO WORRIES. I DON'T CARE.

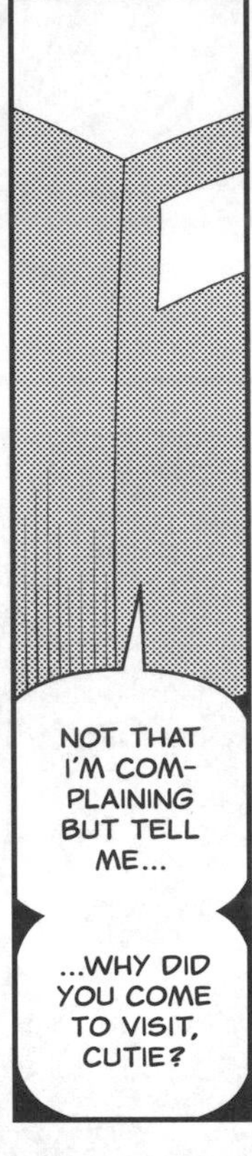
NOT THAT I'M COM-PLAINING BUT TELL ME...
...WHY DID YOU COME TO VISIT, CUTIE?

C-C-CUTIE?
W-WELL, I WANTED-- I WANT TO TALK TO YOU ABOUT...

ABOUT... WELL... ABOUT **THAT** THING!

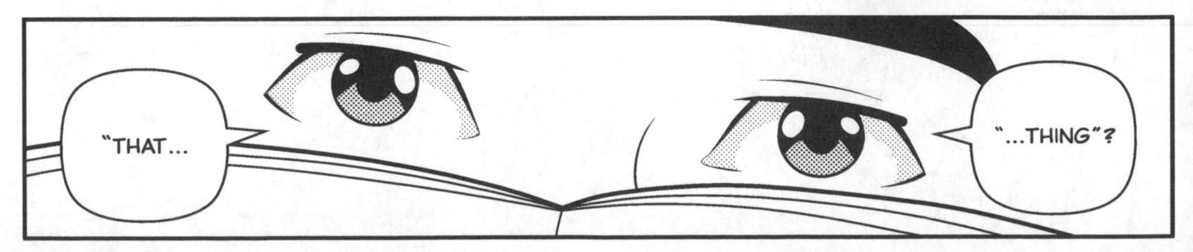
"THAT...
"...THING"?

WE'VE BEEN THROUGH A LOT TOGETHER.
AND SURE, YOU ANNOY ME **A LOT**...

...BUT YOU ALSO SURPRISED ME.
MORE THAN ONCE, WHEN I NEEDED HELP...
...YOU WERE THERE FOR ME.

SO... AFTER EVERYTHING THAT HAPPENED BETWEEN US...
...I THOUGHT A LOT ABOUT IT AND MADE A **DECISION**.

ABOUT HOW THINGS STAND BETWEEN US RIGHT NOW!
BETWEEN ME AND YOU...

NICK NOPE!

AND I'VE DECIDED THAT...
BUT... WAIT! WAIT A MINUTE!
IT DIDN'T HAPPEN THIS WAY!

IT CAN'T! NO WAY! IT'S NOT POSSIBLE!

THE STORY MUST START AT THE BEGINNING BEFORE ARRIVING AT THE END!

I THINK STARTING AT THE END IS MUCH MORE **IMPACTFUL**!
RIGHT TO THE ACTION! NO BEATING AROUND THE BUSH!
UM... H-HI!? I'M RIGHT HERE.
WELL THEN, START AT THE END AND END AT THE BEGINNING!
YOU SEE? SUPER ORIGINAL!
BUT... IT ***CAN'T*** *END NOW!*
EVERY VOLUME IS ONE HUNDRED TWENTY-EIGHT PAGES!

NOOO! NOBODY STARTS A GRAPHIC NOVEL AT THE END! THAT'S CRAZY!
OH, PLEASE! WHAT ABOUT JAPANESE MANGA, HUH?

NOOOOOOOPE...
You got it all backwards!!! You can't read this comic if you start from here. I understand that the original Japanese manga is read in the traditional right to left style... But I had a little conversation with Mauricio and he let us keep our stories the way we are accustomed to - from left to right. Let's agree that even though these comics have a manga style that we respect very much, there is still much of the original Monica's Gang in them too.
Enjoy!!!
Monica
THIS BOOK EVEN HAS A WARNING ON THE LAST PAGE SO PEOPLE DON'T START AT THE BACK LIKE MANGA!
HE'S RIGHT, YOU KNOW.

COPYING AND IMITATION GETS NOWHERE.
THE TRICK IS TO **INNOVATE**!
OH, WELL THEN...

...YOU WANT TO BE **JUST LIKE** *MANGA?*

YOU WANT TO BE JUST LIKE THE **HUNDREDS OF THOUSANDS** *OF OTHER MANGA?*

THAT'S SCREWED UP! EVEN WHEN IT'S **MY** STORY...
...THEY DON'T LET ME DO ANYTHING THE WAY I WANT TO DO IT!
OH, YEAH? TRY HAVING A COMIC WHERE YOU ARE TEASED THE WHOLE TIME!
NEVERTHELESS, **MONICA AND FRIENDS** *ARE CLASSICS!*
NOW, LET'S RETURN TO THE NATURAL ORDER OF THINGS...

WAIT, WHAT? THIS IS NATURAL ORDER?!
STARCH INDUSTRIES
NOW TO SCREW IN THE WHATCHAMA-CALLIT...
...AND ATTACH IT ON, JUST SO, TO THE SUB-FUSES OF THE BRIDGE!

AND WITH A RECALIBRATION OF THE DISTAL SPIRE OF THE INCIDENT CYLINDER, LET'S--
MISTER STARCH! I KNOW THAT YOU ARE... HMM... BUSY...

...BUT YOU HAVE THAT MEETING WITH THE COMPANY SHAREHOLDERS, SIR!

AH, **MISS PAPRIKA**... HAVE THEM APPLY ALL SHARES TO THE **NONETENDO**!
I'M GOING TO MAKE A NEW **GAME** FOR THEM TO GET RICHER!
BUT... BUT, **ANTONIO**, SIR...

BRING ME ANOTHER COFFEE WHILE YOU'RE AT IT!
THIS IS AN IMPORTANT INVENTION! I CAN'T STOP...

...EVEN IF AN ATTACK MISSILE FALLS ON MY HEAD!

KABLAM

AH! THAT WAS CLOSE!
AND PAPRIKA THOUGHT A **FORCE SHIELD** WAS A DUMB INVENTION.
JUST BECAUSE I GOT THE IDEA FROM A CARTOON, **DRAGON'S TAVERN**...

SOMEONE DESTROYED MY FOUR HUNDRED BILLION DOLLAR LAB!
DISRUPTED MY SURVEY OF THE COMPRESSION SHAFT TENSIONER.
AND EVEN WORSE...

...THEY ALMOST KILLED MY LAB RATS! WHAT VILLAINY!
AND HERE I THOUGHT A LIFE OF RESEARCH WAS CALM...
I WON'T FORGIVE WHOEVER DID THIS!
AND I BET I KNOW WHO IT WAS...
YES, ANTONIO STARCH! IT WAS I...
DOCTOR DESTRUCTION!

YOU KNOW THAT NAME IS **EXTREMELY** CORNY, RIGHT?
EVEN FOR A SUPER VILLAIN.
QUIET! YOU DON'T HAVE THE RIGHT TO JUDGE ME!

YOU FIRED ME OFF YOUR RESEARCH TEAM!
YOU MADE ME LOSE EVERYTHING! **EVERYTHING!**

IT WAS ALL **YOUR** FAULT, ACTUALLY.
YOU LET GAMAGUCHI RAYS LEAK ONTO **BRYCE BANANA.** HE GOT ANGRY.
DO YOU KNOW WHAT HAPPENS WHEN HE GETS ANGRY?
I AM NOT THAT WEAKLING WHO BENDS AT YOUR COMMAND!
WITH THIS SUIT, I HAVE THE POWER TO **SMASH** YOU!

SO THAT'S HOW IT IS? IF YOU BROUGHT YOUR TOY...

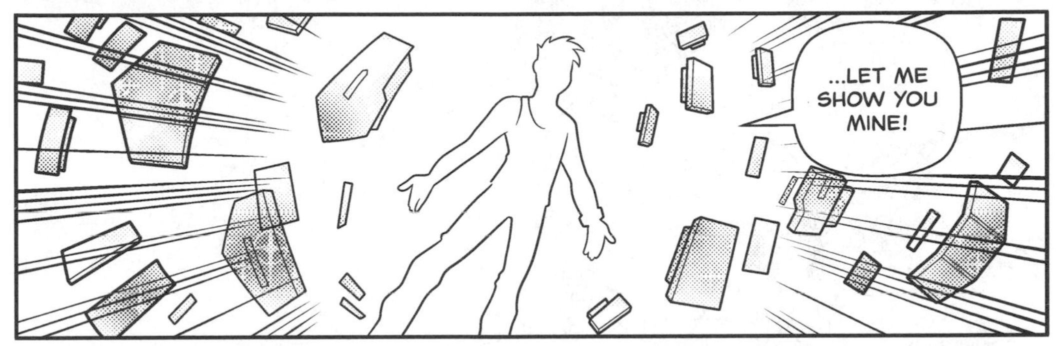
...LET ME SHOW YOU MINE!

TCHING

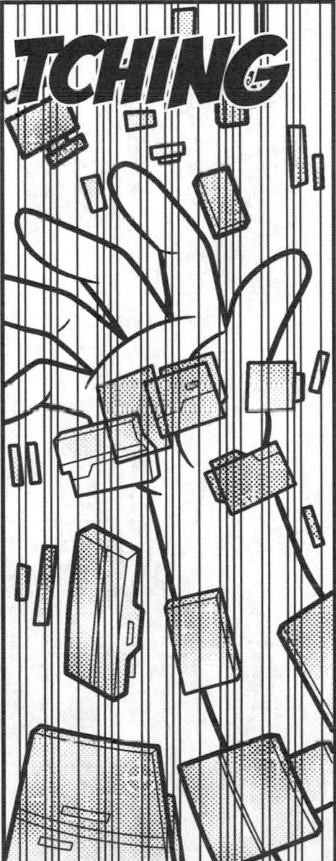
TCHING

TCHINNG

GOLDEN ARMOR!
KNOWLEDGE IS POWER!

HOW SAD. YOU SAY THAT MY NAME IS CORNY...
...BUT YOUR BATTLE CRY EMBARRASSES ME!
I AM AN INVENTOR NOT A MARKETING PRO!

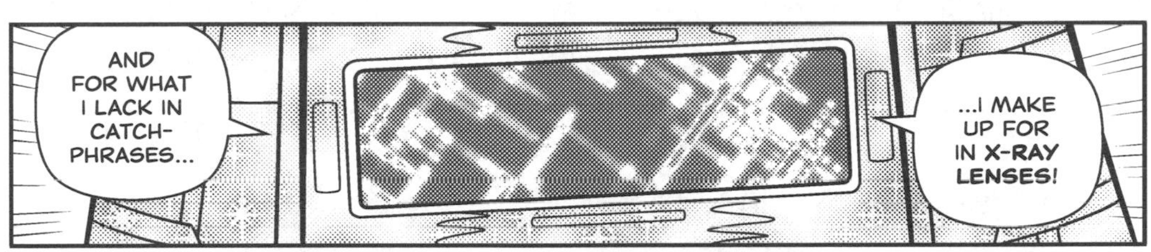
AND FOR WHAT I LACK IN CATCH-PHRASES...
...I MAKE UP FOR IN **X-RAY LENSES!**

INSECT BOXERS, DOCTOR?
THAT'S WHY YOU'RE ALONE!
X-RAY
WHAT?! HOW DO YOU KNOW?

LET'S SEE YOU BE BRAVE...
...WHEN I DEACTIVATE YOUR **POP-UP BLOCKER!**

→ARGH!← NOT THAT!
SPAM KEEPS POPPING UP ON MY SCREEN!
I CAN'T SEE!

MISTER STARCH, HERE IS YOUR COFFEE.
BUT YOU KNOW HOW I HATE WHEN YOU HANG UP IN MY FACE AND--

OOPS! IS THIS A BAD TIME?

PAPRIKA! GET OUT!
AH-HA! NOW I KNOW THE TRUE WEAK POINT OF THE GOLDEN ARMOR!
PITY YOU CAN'T SEE...

...WHAT I WILL DO WITH YOUR LITTLE LADY!
SHOO! BUG OFF!

ZAP
ARGH!
YOU HEARD THE WOMAN, DOCTOR!

WHAT?! YOU CAN SEE?
IMPOSSIBLE! HOW DID YOU BEAT MY VIRUS SO FAST?

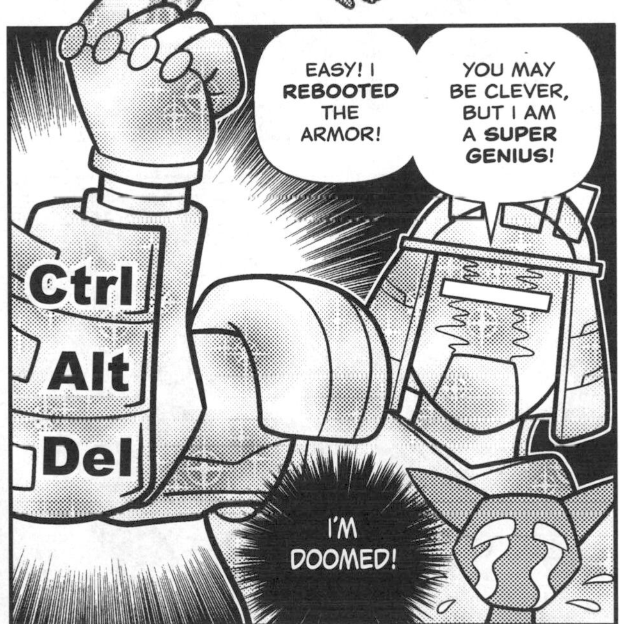
EASY! I **REBOOTED** THE ARMOR!
YOU MAY BE CLEVER, BUT I AM A **SUPER GENIUS!**
Ctrl
Alt
Del
I'M DOOMED!

AAAAAAAAAHHHHHH!

DUDE... **HOLY COW!**
I DIDN'T THINK A SUPERHERO MOVIE COULD BE SO... **SUPER!**
BETTER THAN SUPER! **ULTRA! MEGA! GIGA!**

NO... NO WORDS CAN DESCRIBE IT!
THAT GOLDEN ARMOR IS **WICKED AWESOME!**
THE EFFECTS... THE ACTION...

I COULD FEEL THE RAYS DETONATING BAD GUYS INCHES FROM MY FACE!
OKAY, I **DIDN'T** FEEL IT BUT IT WAS STILL WICKED AWESOME.

COME ON! DIDN'T THE 3-D EFFECTS MAKE YOU SQUIRM IN YOUR SEAT, BROTHER?

ZZZZZZZZZZZ...

NICK NOPE!

OOPS! 'SUP, NIMBUS? DID I MISS ANYTHING?
NO, NOTHING... JUST THE WHOLE MOVIE!

NO BIG DEAL.
WHAT A LAME, BORING FLICK...
WHAT DO YOU MEAN?! ARE YOU NUTS?

IT WAS THE MOST EXCITING CINEMATIC JOURNEY EVER!
THE EFFECTS! THE ACTION! THE EFFECTS! THE CAST! THE EFFECTS!
MAGICIANS LOVE SPECIAL EFFECTS...

REALLY? I DISAGREE...
HOW DO YOU KNOW? YOU SLEPT THE WHOLE TIME.

A GUY AND A GIRL LIKE EACH OTHER, BUT THEY GET IN A FIGHT...
THE GUY GETS SOME POWERS. THEN COMES A VILLAIN WITH OTHER POWERS.
THEY BATTLE. **CRASH! BA-DOOM! SNIKT!**
GOOD DEFEATS EVIL. THE GIRL AND THE GUY MAKE UP.
THE END.
HMM... THAT'S ACTUALLY HOW IT WENT, YEAH...
OF COURSE IT WAS!
SUPERHERO MOVIES ARE ALWAYS LIKE THAT. **PREDICTIBLE**.
EXCUSE ME, SIR!
THIS IS THE **ENTRANCE**. THE EXIT IS THAT WAY.
I KNOW. BUT I WANTED--
I'LL TAKE HIM THERE, SIR.

EX-PEOPL
GOLDEN ARMOR THE MOVIE
THEATRES 1 to 8
SOLD OUT
I CAN'T BELIEVE YOU DIDN'T LIKE **ANYTHING** ABOUT THE MOVIE!
REALLY, DUDE! MAKE AN EFFORT!
YOU CAN'T POSSIBLY BE **THAT** CAPTIOUS.
HMM... LET ME THINK...
AH, I KNOW! I REMEMBER ONE COOL PART...

REMEMBER WHEN THE ARMOR BUMPED INTO THE BAD GUY IN THE MIDDLE OF A **SHOW?**
I THINK THAT WAS RIGHT BEFORE I FELL ASLEEP...
YESS! THAT SCENE WAS **THE BEST!**
THE VILLAIN TAKES HIM TOTALLY BY SURPRISE, BECAUSE HE STILL DOESN'T HAVE COMPLETE CONTROL OF HIS ARMOR AND--

YEAH, RIGHT THEN, WHEN THE GUITARIST IN THE BAND RUNS OFF...
...THE GUITAR HE LEAVES BEHIND...

...IS A FENTER 1979, BRO!
10 QUARTS OF SHAME

YOU'RE KIDDING, RIGHT?
THE ONLY THING YOU LIKED ABOUT THE MOVIE WAS **THAT?**
PAY ATTENTION! A FENTER '79 IS SUPER RARE!
I NEVER SAW ONE SO CLOSE BEFORE.
AT LEAST THE 3-D GLASSES WERE GOOD FOR SOMETHING.

AND REALLY, YOU HAVE A TRACK RECORD OF BEING CONTRARY.
YOU'RE JUST HATING ON THE **MAGIC** OF CINEMA.
"HATING"? I SAID I **LIKED** THE FENTER '79 CLOSE-UPS.

IF YOU WANT TO LOOK AT IT THAT WAY, ALL HEROES ARE ALIKE.
EVEN MORE IN THE COMICS.

REALLY? LET ME SEE...
HAVE YOU HEARD OF ANOTHER COMIC ABOUT A BUCK-TOOTHED GIRL WHO HITS PEOPLE WITH A PLUSH RABBIT?
HUH... NOPE!

AND A BOY WHO LISPS AND WANTS TO TAKE OVER THE WORLD?
ANOTHER WHO WON'T TAKE A BATH?
A GIRL WHO EATS A LOT?
OKAY! OKAY! I GET IT!

A HERO WHO USES MAGIC ATTACKS?
UFF! THIS IS VERY COMMON.
YOU HAVE MENDRAKE, DR. STRANGER, ZANTERRA, ZANTARO, AND...

WHAT ARE YOU INSINUATING?
WHO, ME? NOT A THING...

I'VE GOT TO GET GOING. I HAVE PRACTICE WITH THE BAND.
THEY SCHEDULED FOR FIVE SO J-FIVE'S DAD CAN PICK US ALL UP.

YOU'RE EARLY! IT'S NOT EVEN FOUR.
I KNOW. I'M TAKING THE BUS.
LATER, BRO.

SERI-OUSLY, NICK...
YOUR DESIRE TO ALWAYS BE SO NEGATIVE...

...COULD GET YOU IN TROUBLE.

I HEARD IT WAS REVOLU-TIONARY.
IT'S BEEN AT THE TOP OF THE BOX OFFICE FOR EIGHT WEEKS.
I DON'T LIKE FANTASY MOVIES...
...BUT I HEAR SO MUCH ABOUT THIS THAT I WANT TO SEE IT!

HOW SILLY...
SEEING EVERYONE GETTING IN LINE, LIKE LEMMINGS...

...JUST TO SEE THE MOVIE OF THE MOMENT.
WITHOUT KNOWING WHAT IT'S ABOUT.

ARE YOU KIDDING ME?
I GOTTA GET OUTTA HERE.
I CAN'T STAND THIS SMELL! **GROSS**!

WAIT... I KNOW THAT SMELL...
...IT'S NOT JUST STALE POPCORN!

OH, HOW EMBAR-RASSING!
I **TOLD YOU** TO TAKE A SHOWER BEFORE COMING!
BUT I DID!
I JUST FORGOT TO CHANGE MY CLOTHES ALL WEEK...

SMUDGE!
HUH? WHO? ME? NOOOOO!
I AM... HIS **EVIL TWIN**.

EVIL TWIN, HUH? GOT IT...
DOES HE HAVE AN **EVIL GIRLFRIEND** TOO?

OF COURSE! WE **SPLIT** HER, SEE?
IT'S A MODERN RELATIONSHIP, NOT A BALL AND CHAIN THING...
"SPLIT" ME?
HOW ABOUT I SPLIT **YOUR FACE**, HUH?

SO IT IS JUST A **COINCIDENCE** YOU'RE HERE...

...JUST WHEN SMUDGE **SHOULD** BE GETTING READY FOR BAND PRACTICE?
TOTAL EMBAR- RASS- MENT
OF COURSE. EVIL CLONES DON'T PRACTICE OR SING.
JUST IN MUSICALS OR ON PIRATE SHIPS...

SO YOU MEAN THE REAL SMUDGE WILL BE THERE AT THE RIGHT TIME?

OF COURSE HE WILL. HE IS THE GOOD AND OBEDIENT SMUDGE.

BAH! DISAPPOINT- ING.
IT WAS TOO GOOD TO BE TRUE.
LATER, EVIL TWIN.

HEY, WAIT. WHAT DO YOU MEAN BY THAT?
WELL, EVERYONE COMPLAINS BECAUSE I'M ALWAYS LATE OR EARLY.

I **DETEST** PUNCTUALITY. THE ELEMENT OF SURPRISE IS ESSENTIAL IN THE LIFE OF AN INDIVIDUAL.
WHEN I SAW YOU IN LINE, I THOUGHT SMUDGE WOULD BE LATE FOR PRACTICE.
I THOUGHT, "SMUDGE **GETS ME.**" I WAS **PROUD** OF HIM.

BUT IF THE REAL SMUDGE GETS THERE ON TIME, WHAT'S THE USE?
WE ALL GREW UP AND CHANGED...
...BUT THIS ONE IS STILL INSANE.

ALRIGHT, THEN. I'M OUT.
SAY HI TO EVIL NICK NOPE.
WAIT, NICK. DON'T BE MAD.
DON'T STOP BELIEVING IN ME, MAN.

LET ME SHARE A SECRET...
I AM THE REAL SMUDGE!
ARGH! HIS CRAZINESS IS CONTAGIOUS.

YOU MEAN YOU DON'T HAVE AN EVIL TWIN?
NO WAY. COOL, RIGHT?
HOW COULD YOU?! YOU SKIPPED PRACTICE JUST TO SEE THIS DUMB MOVIE?!

WHAT, NICK? YOU JUST ADMITTED YOU ARE ALWAYS LATE, DUMMY!
SO WHAT? I'M ME, YOU'RE YOU, DUH.
DON'T LOOK AT ME. I HAVE NOTHING TO DO WITH THIS.
I'M JUST THE FRIEND OF THE EVIL GIRLFRIEND FROM A PARALLEL DIMENSION...
ONE MORE THING. DUMB MOVIE, MY FOOT!
GOLDEN ARMOR IS THE MOST FAITHFUL COMICS ADAPTATION OF ALL TIME.
I CRY DURING THE FINAL SCENE EVERY TIME.
"EVERY TIME"? YOU MEAN YOU ARE STANDING UP THE BAND...
...FOR A MOVIE YOU'VE ALREADY SEEN?

TWELVE TIMES.
BUT I PLAN TO BREAK THAT RECORD.
TWELVE?! THIS CRAP?

WHY NOT WAIT FOR THE BLU RAY OR...
TAKE THAT BACK! I AM A DEVOTED FAN OF GOLDEN ARMOR.

I EVEN HAVE THE SUPER RARE ISSUE ZERO COLLECTOR'S EDITION!
AND I WOULD NEVER DEPRIVE MYSELF OF THIS SUBLIME EXPERIENCE IN 3-D!

HOW SUBLIME! COSTUMED GUYS GETTING PUNCHED.
THEY AREN'T COSTUMES! THEY'RE UNIFORMS!

JUST A MINUTE. THERE WASN'T EVEN A SPACE SHIP!
HE'S SUPPOSED TO HAVE A SHIP, FIGHTING ROBOTS, AND--

ARGH!
DON'T CONFUSE GOLDEN ARMOR WITH THE COSMIC WARRIOR!
GOLDEN ARMOR USES ROBOTIC TITAN-STEEL SHIELDS!
THE COSMIC WARRIOR USES A TITAN-STEEL CYBERNETIC JACKET!
THEY ARE COMPLETELY DIFFERENT!

YOU IGNORANT, UNCULTURED BARBARIAN!
AND I THOUGHT FRANKLIN WAS A NERD...

≻AHEM≺... SO THEN, TODAY I BROUGHT MY GIRL TO SEE IT.
I DIDN'T REALLY WANT TO, BUT HE TALKED SO **MUCH** ABOUT IT...

...LET'S BE REAL, THE ACTOR IS REALLY CUTE.
AH! REALLY, SMUDGE?
LOOK AT **DUSTINE** DROOLING OVER THIS GUY?
AREN'T YOU UNCOMFORT-ABLE BY THIS?
NAH! EVEN I'M DROOLING...
LOOK AT THE **PRODUCTION**! THE CHROME SHINE!

HMM... COME TO THINK OF IT...
...IT WOULD BE COOL TO HAVE A GIRLFRIEND WHO LIKES THE SAME THINGS AS ME...

...BUT **NOT** SOME PUNK WITH A FACE LIKE A POST-IT NOTE.

HE DOES NOT HAVE A POST-IT NOTE FACE!
MAYBE A FACE LIKE A 3 SUBJECT NOTEBOOK!
HE DOES, YUP!
NOPE, HE DOESN'T!

HEY... WAITA-MINUTE...
WHERE'D THE LINE GO?

AAAARRGHH!
EVERYONE'S ALREADY INSIDE!

WAIT, GUY! DON'T LOCK US OUT!
LET US IN! THESE TICKETS COST A FORTUNE!
HEY! COME BACK!

YOU CAN'T ESCAPE THE DEBATE.
WHERE IS YOUR HONOR?

● ● ● ● ● ●

I DIDN'T WANT TO DEBATE ANYWAYS...

LET'S LOOK ON THE BRIGHT SIDE.
WITHOUT SMUDGE, THE BAND WILL PLAY **DIFFERENTLY**.
Entrance

AND I LIKE ANYTHING THAT'S DIFFERENT.
GREAT! NOW TO PAY THE BUS FARE AND...

IN THEATERS
GOLDEN ARMOR THE MOVIE

ON SECOND THOUGHT, I'LL WALK...
IT'S NOT SO FAR. SOME 40 BLOCKS?

GOLDEN ARMOR
THE MOVIE
AND THEY SAID I'M THE ONE EXAGGERATING!

EVERYONE SAYING THEY'VE GROWN, HOW MUCH THEY'VE CHANGED...

BUT THEY TAKE NO SHAME IN IDOLIZING SOME TABLOID STAR.
JUST BECAUSE THE MOVIE IS POPULAR.

IF THE LATEST CRAZE WAS TO HANG A WATERMELON OFF YOUR NECK...
...EVERYONE WOULD DO IT, BECAUSE IT'S **FASHION**.

ABSURD! THAT'S CRAZY! THE NERVE!

HEY! YOU CAME OUT OF NOWHERE.
THAT WAS COOL. DO IT AGAIN?

DON'T CHANGE THE SUBJECT, MISTER. WE AREN'T TALKING ABOUT ME...
...WE'RE TALKING ABOUT YOU AND YOUR **FOOLISH-NESS**!

WATERMELON BELONGS IN THE STOMACH, NOT AROUND THE NECK...
THESE IDEAS ARE DANGEROUS FOR THOSE WITH A WEAK HEAD.

MAGGY! YOU UNDERSTAND ME!

HUH? ARE YOU ALRIGHT?
IF YOU DIDN'T NOTICE, I WAS RAGGING ON YOU.
SURE! *SHH!* IT'S ALL GOOD...

I JUST WANT TO GO TO SOME-WHERE...
...WHERE I DON'T FEEL LIKE **HE** IS WATCHING ME!

ANY SUGGES-TIONS?
HMM. AN ICE CREAM PARLOR?

GREAT! LET'S GO TO THE HAMBURGER JOINT!
UH... FINE?

...SO SMUDGE PREFERRED TO GO SEE THE MOVIE FOR THE THIRTEENTH TIME.
NO WAY!

YOU SEE? WHAT SOMEONE WOULDN'T DO TO STAY IN FASHION...
...EVEN DITCHING THEIR FRIENDS!
THAT REALLY IS INCONSIDER-ATE!
MENU

I DON'T KNOW IF PEOPLE REALLY **LIKE** THE MOVIE...
...OR IF THEY GO JUST BECAUSE "EVERYONE SAYS IT'S GOOD."
TRUE!
MENU

THE MAIN ISSUE IS THAT NOBODY THINKS FOR THEMSELVES ANYMORE...
OF COURSE!

EVERYONE WANTS TO THINK THE SAME AS EVERYONE ELSE...
NO DOUBT!

YOU ARE **SO** RIGHT!

AND YOU AREN'T PAYING ATTENTION TO A **THING** I SAY, HUH?
DEFINITELY!
MENU

YOU KNOW SOMETHING? YOU SHOULD DO A **HUNGER STRIKE**...

...TO GET MEDIA ATTENTION AND DENOUNCE THIS SOCIAL EPIDEMIC.
YEAH, THAT'S A GREAT IDEA AND--
WHAT? ARE YOU NUTS?

OOPS, AM I WRONG?
I THOUGHT YOU'D LIKE IT.
AH, MY BAD.
I'LL ADMIT, I WASN'T LISTENING.

BUT WHY'S IT SO HARD TO PICK WHAT TO ORDER?
YOU ALWAYS DECIDE BETWEEN THE **WHATEVER** OR THE **KITCHEN SINK**!

OH, I AM DOING AN EXPERI-MENT.
I AM TRYING THE **ROBERTO DANIEL JUNIOR** DIET.
ROBERTO WHO?

Your healthy obsess
HUNKS
Dieting with
Roberto
Daniel
Junior
OH, YOU KNOW HIM. HE IS THE ACTOR IN GOLDEN ARMOR!

HE IS THE MOST **HEALTHY** CELEBRITY ON FILM.
HE GOT THE ROLE BY BEING IN GREAT HEALTH AND PHYSICAL CONDITION.
HEALTH?! PHYSICAL CONDITION?!
FOR WHAT?! HE SPENDS ALL HIS TIME **INSIDE A TIN CAN!**

I READ THE MAGAZINES AND SITES THAT TALK ABOUT HIS EXERCISE ROUTINE AND DIET.
I WANT TO SEE IF IT REALLY WORKS OR IF THERE IS SOME KIND OF SECRET.

AND, HONESTLY, THE ACTOR IS REALLY A HUNK.

THE **BEST** PART?
THIS RESTAURANT HAS A **COMBO** THAT COMES WITH FREE MOVIE TICKETS AND--

HUH? **NICK NOPE?** WHERE'RE YOU GOING?!

L-LATER, MAGGY...
I LOST MY APPETITE. MY STOMACH IS FEELING FUNNY.

THIS MUST BE A JOKE.
THERE'S NO WAY THE GOLDEN ARMOR CAN BE EVERY-WHERE!

HI, NICK NOPE! WHAT'S UP?

UGH! THE UNIVERSE IS MESSING WITH ME!

OKAY, GET OUT, LITTLE MISS METAL!
DON'T CALL ME THAT!
OR ELSE I WILL SHOOT MY HAIR LOSS RAYS, J-BALDY!

I DON'T KNOW WHAT'S WORSE...
A KID SCARING EVERYONE WITH THE OLD MASK TRICK...
...OR ME FALLING FOR IT!

HEY, NOPE. YOU LOOK LIKE YOU SAW A GHOST.
HAVEN'T YOU NOTICED?
THE CITY IS TAKEN OVER BY THIS GOLDEN ARMOR THING!

HIS FACE IS EVERY-WHERE!
SOMETIMES I THINK I AM SEEING DOUBLE AND--

HERE COMES GOLDEN GIRL AND HER EVER-PRESENT EMERALD DOG...
..TO HER MYSTERIOUS PET SHOP WORLD, WHERE THE SUPER GROOMER AWAITS!
"EVER-PRESENT DOG"?! HE WASN'T EVEN IN THE LAST TWO GRAPHIC NOVELS!
ANYTHING TO MAKE A JOKE, HUH?
THAT'S BECAUSE WE LEAVE HIM OUT BACK, SEE?

WE'LL BE BACK, SON!
THEN I'LL DROP YOU ALL OFF AFTER PRACTICE!
THANKS, DAD!

BAND PRACTICE? WAITASEC!
YOU'RE HERE! AND YOUR DAD! WITH THE CAR!
THAT CAN'T MEAN...

IT'S ALREADY FIVE O'CLOCK?!
I RAN SO MUCH THAT I MANAGED TO ARRIVE PUNCTUALLY?
NOOO! THIS IS IMPOSSIBLE!
HMM... ACTUALLY...
..THERE'S STILL FIVE MINUTES UNTIL FIVE!

-AHEM!- NOT AS BAD.
INSTANT RECUPERATION
WHAT A SAD THING. A LIFE DEDICATED TO A CAUSE...

...GIVING IT UP TO SOME CHEAP ACTION STAR OF SOME SCRAP METAL HERO!
EH... I HAVE NO IDEA WHAT YOU ARE TALKING ABOUT.

I AM TALKING ABOUT THE **DANGER** THAT THIS DUDE REPRESENTS.
HE IS **TAKING OVER MINDS**! CAUSING WAVES OF **COLLECTIVE HYSTERIA**! AND EVEN WORSE...

...HE ALMOST MADE ME **PREDICT-ABLE**!
HE TRIED TO UNDO THE **UNDOABLE LAWS** OF NATURE!

WHAT? YOU ARRIVING ON TIME VIOLATES SOME KIND OF LAW?
WHAT LAW IS THAT? THE LAW OF **TOTAL CONTRARIAN-ISM**?

NOT NECES-SARILY!
THAT SAYS IT ALL!

I CAN SEE THE HEADLINES NOW:
GOLDEN ARMOR: HERO OR MENACE?
HEE-HEE! ALL THIS REVOLT BECAUSE ARMOR IS IN FASHION FOR A MINUTE?

YOU ARE VERY NAÏVE, NOPE!
YOU GO AGAINST WHAT THE MAJORITY LIKES, JUST BECAUSE YOU LIKE THE CONFLICT.

I CAN GET YOU ENJOYING A CHALLENGE...
...BUT THINK OF THE ADVANTAGES OF BEING ON THE SAME SIDE AS OTHERS!

ADVAN-TAGES?
YUP! WANNA SEE?

'SUP, LADIES?
HI, J-FIVE...

AH! STOP! STOP EVERY-THING!
OH, MY STARS, DENISE! WHAT HAPPENED?

YOU HAVE TO ASK, CARMEN BABE?
LOOK AT THE GOLDEN AURA RADIAT-ING FROM THIS YOUNG FACE!
FEEL THE VIBES OF SUCCESS EMANATING FROM EVERY STEP!

THIS BEEFCAKE WOKE UP TODAY AND SAID...
"GET UP AND CRUSH IT!"
DENISE HAS A POINT, J.
THERE'S SOMETHING DIFFERENT ABOUT YOU...

AHHH! I KNOW!
THIS LOOK THAT YOU HAVE TODAY...

...IT'S THE SAME AS ROBERTO DANIEL JUNIOR!
YES! IT'S A HOLLYWOOD SUPER-TREND!

THEY'RE RIGHT, J-FIVE. YOU LOOK REALLY GOOD IN THAT.
SEE? HE HAS THE TASTE TO TRY STYLE!
NOT EVERYONE CAN, YOU KNOW?

ISN'T THIS THE SAME AS HIS CHARACTER IN THE MOVIE?
ROBERTO DANIEL JUNIOR AND THE ARMOR ARE ONE ENTITY, **MARINA!**

IT'S RARE TO SEE BOYS DRESSING SO GOOD EVERY DAY.
I LOVE THE PRODUCTION, CUTIE.
AH, GIRLS! CUT IT OUT!

I DIDN'T EVEN THINK OF THIS WHEN I GOT DRESSED TODAY...
TOTAL EMBARRASSMENT SQUARED!

MY BAD, LADIES, BUT I GOT TO GO NOW!
BAND PRACTICE, YOU KNOW HOW IT IS...
BYE AND CON-GRATS!
I WANT TO SEE YOU EXPLODE IN THE **FASHION** WORLD, YOU HEAR? #PROUD!

TA-DAH! YOU SEE?
WHAT DO YOU THINK OF MY PERFORMANCE, NICK NOPE?

DON'T COME ANY CLOSER! STAY FAR AWAY! KEEP YOUR DISTANCE!
GOLDEN ARMOR'S BRAINLESS FANS...
YOU'RE ONE OF THEM!
COME ON, DON'T BE NUTS! IT'S NOTHING LIKE THAT.
SURE, THE FILM WAS OKAY...

...BUT I THINK THE PALADIN OF DARKNESS IS MUCH BETTER!
AND THAT ROBERTO DANIEL JUNIOR HAS A BRO FACE...
FOR SOME REASON, I DON'T LIKE THIS CONTRADIC-TION.
SO, YOU DON'T LIKE THE MOVIE? OR THE ACTOR?

NICK NOPE, HERE'S THE SECRET...
YOU DON'T REALLY NEED TO FOLLOW THE TRENDS.

YOU JUST NEED TO SEEM LIKE YOU ARE. TO GET THE ATTENTION OF OTHERS.
BEING POPULAR GETS YOU FAR IN LIFE!
IF THE WARDROBE OF THIS DUDE GETS ME ADMIRED, SO BE IT.
IT DOESN'T MATTER WHAT I THINK OF HIM.

GET IT? DEEP DOWN, I'M A REBEL LIKE YOU!
BUT INSTEAD OF GOING AROUND JUDGING EVERYONE...

YOU SHOULD BE LIKE ME!
AGREEING JUST ON THE OUTSIDE! FOR APPEAR-ANCES!

THIS WAY YOU CAN KEEP UP WITH TRENDS...
...AND STILL HAVE YOUR UNIQUE PERSONALITY.
IN OTHER WORDS...

YOU THINK I SHOULD LIE ABOUT WHAT I THINK.

LIE IS A STRONG WORD...
OMIT IS MORE LIKE IT!

YOU KNOW SOMETHING, J-FIVE?
I THINK THAT'S **MUCH WORSE** THAN DROOLING OVER SOME SUPERHERO.

AND ANOTHER THING!
YOU AND I AREN'T THAT **ALIKE** AT ALL AND--

HI, GUYS!

HOW IS IT GOING?
HI, MONICA!
BYE, MONICA!

HUH? YOU'RE LEAVING?
NO! IT'S JUST A DIFFERENT WAY OF GREETING YOU!

DID YOU KNOW, IN ITALIAN, CIAO MEANS BOTH HELLO AND--
NO WAY, J-FIVE!

YOU ARE THE ONE WHO'S DIFFERENT TODAY!
LIKE... ALL STYLISH!
LEFT IN THE VOID

AH... GLAD YOU LIKE IT!
TOLD YOU!

BUT AREN'T YOU A BIT DRESSED UP FOR A REHEARSAL?
BESIDES, WHERE IS EVERY-ONE?
RIGHT? SMUDGE SEEMED TO HAVE SOMETHING ELSE TO DO...

...SO I CALLED MAGGY AND CANCELED!
YOU DID WHAT?!

WAIT... YOU ONLY TOLD MAGGY?
J-FIVE! YOU BROUGHT ME HERE JUST TO PLAY A TRICK?!
OF COURSE NOT, SILLY!

SINCE MY DAD'S GIVING US A RIDE ANYWAYS...
...I WANTED TO INVITE YOU TO THE MOVIES!
R-REALLY?

YOU BET! AND YOU PICK THE MOVIE!
FOR REAL?
COULD WE SEE **GOLDEN ARMOR**?

BONK BONK BONK BONK BONK BONK BON

BONK BONK BO K BONK BONK BON
UMM... WHY IS NICK HITTING HIS HEAD ON THAT WALL?
OUCH! DOESN'T THAT HURT?

AH, YOU KNOW HE'S ALWAYS BEEN A BIT **STRANGE**...
LET'S GO, MY DAD WILL BRING US!
J-FIVE... THIS IS GREAT!
YOUR SURPRISE... YOUR NEW STYLE...

I DID IT ALL THINKING OF YOU!

SORRY, BUT I BEG TO DIFFER...

YOU TOLD CARMEN SOMETHING VERY DIFFERENT!
YOU SAID YOU DIDN'T **REALIZE** HOW YOU WERE DRESSED TODAY!
WHAT... YOU DID?
N-NICK NOPE... WHAT DO YOU THINK YOU'RE DOING? YOU--
I'M DOING WHAT I ALWAYS DO...
THE **OPPOSITE** OF WHAT EVERYONE WANTS OF ME.
WAS I SUPPOSED TO KEEP IT A **SECRET**? WELL...

J-FIVE...?
IT'S NOTHING, MO!
I MEANT TO SAY I DIDN'T KNOW IT WAS WORKING... I MEAN...

DON'T BE MODEST. YOUR **CASUAL STYLE** WAS A BIG SUCCESS!
DENISE AND MARINA WERE ALL OVER IT! TELL HER...

YOU WERE SHOWING OFF?! FOR-- FOR MARINA?!
EVEN FOR DENISE?!
HEY! WHAT DO YOU MEAN "EVEN FOR DENISE"?

N-NO WAY, MO! I TOLD YOU I DRESSED LIKE THIS FOR YOU! **YOU**!
SEE? IS IT WORTH IT COPYING THE WARDROBE OF THAT BIGSHOT ACTOR...

...WHO
YOU THINK
HAS A BRO
FACE?
ROBERTO
DANIEL
JUNIOR?
BRO
FACE?

J-FIIIIIIIVVVE!

GRR!
NOW LET'S SEE HIM SHOW OFF FOR ANYONE!
LET'S SEE HIS LOOK WHEN IT'S...
INSIDE OUT!
STOMP

ARGH!
I WANT TO TURN THE REST OF HIM INSIDE OUT!
WHO KNOWS?! MAYBE I WOULD TRULY UNDERSTAND HIM INSIDE OUT!
YOUR WAY SEEMS MORE FUN THAN AN X-RAY...

...BUT THAT WOULDN'T BE AN AGE APPROPRIATE COMIC FOR MANY!

AND YOU! WHAT'S YOUR DEAL, NICK NOPE?
ARE YOU FOOLING ME TOO?
WHO? ME?

WELL, IT'S NOT WORTH TRYING TO CALM ME DOWN, GOT IT?
I DON'T WANT TO CALM DOWN!

I MAY NOT HIT MY PROBLEMS ANYMORE...
...BUT I STILL HAVE THE RIGHT TO BE MAD!
TRY AND CALM YOU DOWN?

WHY WOULD I DO SOMETHING LIKE THAT?

LEMON TREE MALL
GO, MONICA! LET'S SEE!
KNOCK HIM OUT!

TAKE HIM DOWN, MONICA!
FLYING KICK!
UPPER CUT!
K.O.!
NEW WORLD RECORD!

BRLOM
BL-AM

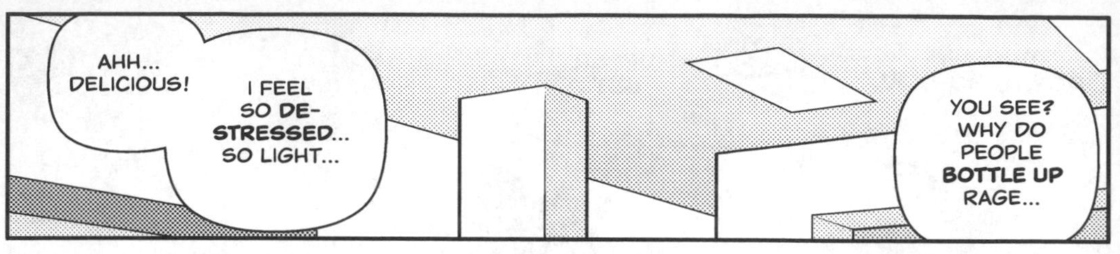
AHH... DELICIOUS!
I FEEL SO DE-STRESSED... SO LIGHT...
YOU SEE? WHY DO PEOPLE BOTTLE UP RAGE...

...IF THERE ARE SO MANY FUN WAYS TO RELEASE IT?
AND THEN FEEL SO GOOD AFTER.

YOU KNOW SOMETHING, NICK? YOUR TILTED HEAD WORKS OUT SOMETIMES.
WHEN-EVER I GET MAD...

...THE FIRST THING EVERYONE DOES IS TRY TO CALM ME DOWN.
I'M NOT EVERYONE.
THEY ONLY DO THAT BECAUSE THEY ARE SCARED...

...AND THEY DON'T REALIZE HOW BEAUTIFUL YOU ARE ANGRY.

UHH... I-I... HEH...
AND **EVEN MORE** BEAUTIFUL WHEN YOU'RE SPEECHLESS.

HAHAHAHAHAHAH
AHAHAHAHAHAHA
HAH... THANKS?
AH, NICK! THERE'S NO ONE QUITE LIKE YOU!
WHY DON'T I FEEL LIKE THAT'S A COMPLIMENT?

IT EVEN SEEMS LIKE YOU **PRETEND** TO GET ME JUST TO WIND ME UP...
...LIKE J-FIVE ALWAYS DOES!

AH, J-FIVE...
HOW DID WE WIND UP TALKING ABOUT HIM, AGAIN?

HE JUST DOESN'T NOTICE! HE'S ALWAYS WITH THE SWEET TALK, THE PLAN, THE SCHEME...
I DON'T KNOW WHY I STILL LISTEN TO WHAT HE SAYS AND...

HUH... WHY'D YOU GET SO QUIET ALL OF A SUDDEN?

BECAUSE, IF I CAN'T DISAGREE...
...BETTER TO NOT SAY ANY-THING.

THE STRONGEST GIRL I KNOW... TOTALLY KICK BUTT!
NO WAY! THAT'S NOT YOU!
WHAT?
B-BUT I DIDN'T SAY--

I HAVE A FRAGILE SIDE. I...
B-BUT... I THOUGHT YOU UNDER-STOOD ME!

ADMIT IT, THIS IS JUST BECAUSE J-FIVE DECEIVED YOU...
...AND, **EVEN STILL,** YOU CAN'T RESIST HIM?

GEE, NICK...
YOU GET ME **MORE** THAN I THOUGHT YOU DID!
IT'S NOT HARD.
I THINK THE OPPOSITE OF WHAT YOU TRY TO DEMON-STRATE.

IT'S A PITY, MONICA.
YOU DESERVE **MORE** THAN THIS!

WELL, YOU'RE **RIGHT**.
I NEED TO BE MORE LIKE YOU. MORE HONEST WITH MYSELF...

I NEED TO FIND SOMEONE WHO I TRULY ADMIRE.
SOMEONE BRAVE... ATTENTIVE... SINCERE...
SOMEONE LIKE...
ME! ME! ME!
ROBERTO DANIEL JUNOR!
THE ACTOR FROM GOLDEN ARMOR!

NOOOOOO!

NO WHAT?
NOT YOU TOO! THE WHOLE WORLD IS STUCK DROOLING OVER HIM.
WHAT'S SO SPECIAL ABOUT THIS GUY? WHAT?

WHAT'S SO SPECIAL? YOU MEAN, ASIDE FROM BEING HANDSOME, CHARISMATIC, TALENTED...
YOU DON'T KNOW ANYTHING ABOUT HIM, HUH?

I DON'T AND I DON'T WANT TO!
DON'T WANT TO, HUH?

IT'S FOR THE BEST. YOU WOULDN'T UNDERSTAND ANYWAY.

WHAT DO YOU MEAN I WOULDN'T UNDERSTAND?
YOU CAN'T JUDGE ME WITHOUT TRYING! TELL ME THE STORY OF THIS DUDE NOW!

ROBERTO DANIEL JUNIOR WAS A COMPLETELY UNKNOWN ACTOR...
HE HAD A NORMAL, MODEST LIFE. FILLED WITH BILLS TO PAY...
BUT I'M JUST THREE MONTHS BEHIND ON RENT.
DO YOU KNOW **WHO** YOU ARE SPEAKING TO?
IF YOU PAY UP, YOU COULD BE **CAPTAIN PITHCO** FOR ALL I CARE.

AUDITIONS
HIS CAREER WAS VERY DIFFICULT.
HE WAS ALWAYS IN LINE FOR AUDITIONS FOR COMMERCIALS, MOVIES, STAGE SHOWS...

...AND THE REST OF THE TIME, HE GOT GIGS AND TEMPORARY JOBS.
"TO BE OR NOT TO BE, THAT IS THE QUESTION..."
NO QUESTION ABOUT IT! THAT'S A STEAK!
BUT WE ORDERED THE **VEGE-TARIAN**!

BUT THE MOST DIFFICULT BATTLE WAS TO COME!
ROBERTO PROVED TO BE A **WARRIOR**! **A SOLDIER**!
YIKES! DID SOME-THING AWFUL HAPPEN TO HIM?!

OH, NAH... HE GOT SOME ROLES IN WAR MOVIES!
PLOP

DESPITE HIS GREAT TALENT...
...HE BECAME A **TERROR** FOR THE FILM CREWS.

THEY SAID HE CREATED A LOT OF MESSES ON SET!
HI, MOMMY!
IT'S NO USE, DIRECTOR. WE HAVE TO RESHOOT THE SCENE...
...FOR THE NINETY SIXTH TIME!
WHY COULDN'T WE GO WITH THAT FORMER CHILD STAR ACTOR? WHY?

NO ONE APPRECIATED THE TALENT THE YOUNG GENIUS DISPLAYED!
MY BAD, GUYS! HOW ABOUT WE TAKE FIVE FOR DRINKS ON ME?
THE RESTAURANT WHERE I WORK IS CLOSE BY AND...

OR RATHER...
ALMOST NO ONE!

THAT NIGHT, THE SPECIAL EFFECTS TEAM ATE WITH HIM.
WHAT AN AWFUL DIRECTOR! I CAN'T EVEN SAY HI TO MY MOMMY?
IF WE CAN'T REMEMBER OUR MOTHERS WHEN WE GET TO THE TOP, WHO CAN WE REMEMBER?
ANYONE WANT A REFILL?

THEY WERE FROM A SMALL TECHNOLOGY COMPANY, ART&TECH.
THEY LIKED SPECIAL EFFECTS AND WANTED TO MAKE THEIR OWN FILM.

BUT THEY DIDN'T HAVE AN ACTOR ATTACHED...
...UNTIL THAT MOMENT.

ROBERTO WAS CHARISMATIC, ATHLETIC, NICE...
...AND MOST IMPORTANTLY... HE WAS SUPER CHEAP TO HIRE.

ROBERTO WAS SO HAPPY! THIS WAS HIS BIG CHANCE IN LIFE!
HE PUT A LOT OF EFFORT INTO IT. HE TRAINED AND REHEARSED SO MUCH FOR THE ROLE.
WHY DO YOU INSIST ON COMING HERE SO MUCH?
THEY ALWAYS GET OUR ORDER WRONG HERE...

SO THEN, ROBERTO DANIEL JUNIOR BECAME **ANTONIO STARCH!**
A GENIUS INVENTOR FROM THE COMICS, WHO USES SAMURAI ARMOR OF STEEL. HE IS THE--
I KNOW! I KNOW! YOU DON'T NEED TO SAY IT **AGAIN!**

SEE, NICK? THAT'S WHY RDJ IS ADMIRED SO MUCH.
HE GOT SO FAR THANKS TO HIS OWN EFFORTS!
RDJ? I THOUGHT JUST J-FIVE HAD THE ONLY ABBREVIATED NAME AROUND HERE!

BAH! HIS CAREER IS JUST PURE LUCK...
...AND ONE DAY, HIS LUCK WILL RUN OUT!

THIS SUPERHERO WILL BE LOST TO TIME...
...JUST LIKE ANY OTHER TREND.
WELL, YOU CAN KEEP ON WISHING FOR THAT.

ART&TECH STARTED A FRANCHISE! THEY ARE PLANNING SEVEN MORE FILMS!
MORE DUMB FILMS WITH LASERS AND INVEN-TIONS?
I GOT IT! THEY'LL GIVE HIM A YOUNG SIDEKICK DRESSED LIKE A CAN OF TUNAFISH...

BETTER! IN THE NEXT MOVIE, THERE WON'T BE JUST ONE HERO...

...BUT A WHOLE LEAGUE OF THEM!
GOLDEN ARMOR AND THE ARMY OF GOLD!
IT WILL BE THE BIGGEST MOVIE OF NEXT YEAR!
I HOPE THE NEW ACTORS ARE HUNKS AS WELL!

THAT'S IT! I'M MOVING TO TIMBUKTU!
WHY? IS THE CINEMA THERE BETTER?

MONICA, DON'T YOU GET IT? THEY ARE LIKE A **PLAGUE**!
THEY ARE **SPREADING! MULTIPLY-ING!**
JUST LIKE A COLD ON A CROWDED BUS.

AND WORSE... **EVERYONE LOVES IT AND CAN'T TALK ABOUT ANYTHING ELSE!**
IT'S LIKE BRAIN-WASHING! HYPNOSIS! MIND CONTROL!
IT COULD EVEN BE SOME PLAN TO...

...TAKE OVER THE WORLD!

HEY! I DON'T LIKE **ANYTHING** ABOUT THAT LOOK!

PARDON ME, SIR! PERHAPS A SEARCH ENGINE WOULD HELP MORE...?
WE HAVE INTERNET ACCESS HERE.
LIBRARY
THANKS, MA'AM. I'M ALRIGHT.

SO THIS DANIEL JUNIOR WAS DISCOVERED BY ART&TECH....
...A SMALL SPECIAL EFFECTS BUSINESS.

BUT WHAT "SMALL BUSINESS" CAN FUND A MOVIE THIS EXPENSIVE?
THERE'S SOMETHING VERY BAD ABOUT THIS...

AH-HA! FOUND IT!
QUIET!

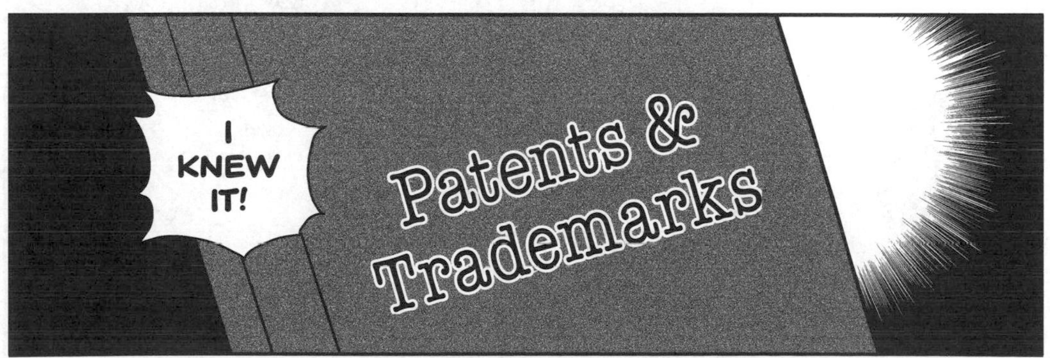
I KNEW IT!
Patents & Trademarks

EXTRA! EXTRA!
HUH? WHAT'S GOING ON HERE?

GOLDEN ARMOR! HERO OR MENACE?
NICK NOPE REVEALS THE TRUTH!

AGAIN WITH THIS STUPID THEORY?
NOW IT'S PROVEN! HERE'S THE PROOF!

WHAT THE--?! THE G.A. MOVIE IS A PLAN FOR WORLD DOMINATION?
SLANDER! DEFAMATION! HE IS A HERO, MAN!

READ THE PAMPHLET CAREFULLY, SMUDGE.
LOOK HERE! IT SAYS THAT THE ARMOR WAS AN OLD ART&TECH PROJECT...

ARMY&TECH
...BUT THE BOOK OF PATENTS AND TRADEMARKS SAYS OTHER-WISE.
THIS PATENT BELONGS TO ONE ARMY&TECH!

IT'S A SECURITY COMPANY THAT CHANGED ITS NAME.
THEY MAKE COMBAT EQUIPMENT.

SO, THEY CHANGED THEIR PLANS. BIG WHOOP.
MY DAD'S CHANGED JOBS THREE TIMES!

ARGH!
HOW IS IT POSSIBLE YOU GOT NOTHING FROM THAT?
IT'S A BIG CONSPIR-ACY!

THE GOLDEN ARMOR IS A SECRET WEAPON TO TAKE OVER THE WORLD!

HAHAHAHAHAHAHAHAHAHAHAHAHAHAHAHAHAHAHAHAHAH
AHAHAHAHAHAHAHAHAHAHAHAHAHAHAHAHAHAHAHAHA
IT'S NOT FUNNY!
THIS IS SLANDER! DEFAMATION!
POOR GOLDEN ARMOR...

AH, YOU'RE OVER-DOING IT A BIT!
IF THE WEAPON IS A SECRET, WHY MAKE A MOVIE ABOUT IT?
IT'S THE **LEAST OBVIOUS** WAY TO CONTROL PEOPLE, LOGICALLY.
THAT'S WHY I WAS THE FIRST TO FIND OUT!

THEY EVEN HIRED A **POSTER BOY** TO MAKE EVERYONE LIKE THE IDEA.
SOMEONE "HANDSOME, CHARISMATIC, AND TALENTED" LIKE...

ROBERTO DANIEL JUNIOR!
BLEARGH! JUNIOR ROBERTO DANIEL!

NOT ME, MISS. I'M NICK NOPE!
LIKE I DON'T KNOW THAT, YOU DIMWIT?
ONLY YOU WOULD GO MAKING A BIG DEAL OF THIS DUMB IDEA!

ENOUGH, OKAY? IT'S BEST TO STOP NOW BEFORE THINGS GET SERIOUS.
COME ON! HOW COME NICK ALWAYS ACTS OUT...
...BUT NEVER GETS ON MONICA'S NERVES?

NO, MONICA. NOTHING'S GOING TO STOP ME FROM UNEARTHING THIS EVIL PLAN!
THE TRUTH IS HERE INSIDE!

OUT THERE! THE TRUTH IS OUT THERE!
Y-FILES THEME SONG
NO! IT'S HERE INSIDE OF MY HEAD!
AND I NEED TO SHARE IT WITH THE WORLD, AND--

NICK, MY CHERUB OF THE CONTRARY! THERE YOU ARE!

THIS IS ALL CONFIDENTIAL, BUT TELL A GIRL...
REAL OR FAKE NEWS? DID YOU REALLY MAKE THESE SUPER FASHIONABLE GOLDEN ARMOR STATIONERY?

STATIONERY?! THOSE ARE PAMPHLETS!
UNEARTHING THE BIGGEST MARKETING SCAM OF THE CENTURY!
SCORE! IT WAS HIM, LADIES!

SO, IT'S YOU GOING AROUND SLANDERING ROBERTO DANIEL JUNIOR?

AND THEY STILL ASK WHY I'M WITH THIS GIRL!
THAT IS WHAT I MEANT BY "GETTING SERIOUS"!

I HATE STOOPING TO CON-VENTIONAL MEANS.
BUT NOW I AM PART OF THE **SECRET RESISTANCE**...

...I HAVE TO PROTECT MY INTEGRITY!
I WILL REVEAL ALL WITH A BLOG POST ON MY SITE.
Nick's Nopes

HEY! ALREADY PEOPLE ARE COMMENTING ON IT!

Blog says:
FIRRRRSSST! I w@s 1st! l8r!

Carmen says:
Ur just jealous because he has 3 names and you just have alliteration.

Maria Angela says:
WEEEEEEE! :PPPP

J-Five says:
You're Nuts!

Professor
Ned Says:
I AM NOT
CRAZY!

Smudge says:
o-/-<]:

Maggy says:
The body should
be healthy, but so
should the mind!

Bucky says:
Go see a
doctor!

Marina says:
Diploma
Doctor

Denise says:
UR lit, divine,
absolute and mul-
timedia, visit my
Insta 4 more affir-
mations.
The De list!
XOXO LUV YA! MUAH!

Nimbus says:
GET OFF MY
COMPUTER!

Monica says:
Nick, please...
give up this
insane idea.

DON'T LET THEM FOOL YOU!

THE HERO THAT YOU ALL LOVE IS REALLY A VILLAIN!

THE GOLDEN ARMOR SOUNDTRACK IS PRETTY SWEET, HUH?
HELLO? WHAT DID I TELL YOU?

CAREFUL! THAT IS THE SOUNDTRACK TO WORLD DOMINATION!
ARGH! WHERE ARE MY HEAD-PHONES?

HA! YOU CAN'T ESCAPE THE TRUTH!
THEY CAN'T STAY LISTENING TO MUSIC ALL DAY!

OR COULD THEY?

I CAME HERE TO SHARE THIS SONG...

HERE'S THE STORY OF A HERO
WHO IS REALLY A VILLAIN
GOL-DEN AR-MOR
MORE HOLES IN HIS STORY
AND MAKING A KILLING!

YOU WANT TO HEAR THE GOLDEN ARMOR SONG?
WELL, TAKE THIS!

TAKE THIS, YOU BRATTY KID!

NICK NOPE! ARE YOU OKAY?!

DENISE TOLD ME THEY THREW WATER ON YOU.
DENISE WOULD. AND THEY COMPLAIN WHEN I THINK EVERYONE IS **PREDICTABLE...**

FOR REAL! YOU NEED TO STOP MAKING PEOPLE UNCOMFORT-ABLE.
DON'T YOU SEE HOW THINGS ARE GETTING OUT OF HAND?

NO BIG DEAL.
IT'S SO HOT OUT, I NEEDED TO COOL DOWN ANYWAYS.

IT JUST STINKS THAT THEY CON-FISCATED MY DRUMS...

...BECAUSE I DIDN'T HAVE A PERMIT TO DO A **PUBLIC** SHOW.
YOU COULD HAVE PUT YOUR MUSIC ON THE INTERNET.
THAT'S A LOT **SAFER!**

THAT'S IT! I STILL HAVE BAGPIPES, TWO BONGOS, AND A TRIANGLE!
I CAN EVEN TURN OFF THE COMMENTS.
NICK NOPE! KNOCK IT OFF! LISTEN TO ME!

THE **MORE** NOISE YOU MAKE...
...THE **LESS** PEOPLE WANT TO HEAR IT.

THAT'S DUE TO THE **BRAIN-WASHING** OF GOLDEN ARMOR!
IT SEEMS LIKE WITCHCRAFT!
OH! THAT'S WHY NIMBUS KEEPS BLABBING ABOUT THE MAGIC OF CINEMA...

BUT I STILL **DON'T AGREE** WITH YOU!
WHAT A SHOCK...

YOU SAID THAT NO ONE PAYS ATTENTION TO ME, BUT THAT'S **NOT** TRUE.
SOME-BODY CARES A **LOT** ABOUT WHAT I SAY.
OH, YEAH? WHO?

OBVIOUSLY, I'M WORRIED! GOSH!
NO ONE PULLS CRAZY STUNTS LIKE THIS!
WEARING OUT THE PATIENCE OF THE WHOLE WORLD! YOU'LL GET **HURT**!

YOU JUST WANT THE RIGHT TO SPEAK YOUR MIND. SAY WHAT YOU BELIEVE IN.
BUT I KNOW YOU **DIDN'T WANT** TO BUG ANYONE.

YOU ARE SOMEONE WHO DOESN'T HIDE YOUR...

...FEELINGS.

THANKS, MONICA!
THAT MEANS A LOT TO ME!

Y-YOU MEAN YOU'LL HEAR ME OUT?

I'LL DO THE **OPPOSITE**! THE MORE YOU INSIST...
...THE MORE I AM DETERMINED TO KEEP GOING!
-SIGH!- AND THEY SAY THAT **I'M** STUBBORN!

MY BIGGEST PROBLEM IS THAT I'M SO USED TO CONTRADICTING...
...THAT I DON'T KNOW HOW TO GET PEOPLE TO HEAR ME!

I NEED SOME HELP! SOMEONE WHO EVERYONE TRUSTS.
SOMEONE WHO EVERY-ONE ADMIRES AND RESPECTS.

I NEED ROBERTO JUNIOR DANIEL!
WHAT?!

WAITASEC! DIDN'T YOU SAY HE WAS A VILLAIN?
THAT THIS IS JUST AN EVIL SCHEME, ETC., ETC.?

SO YOU BELIEVE ME?
YOU'RE CONTRA-DICTING YOURSELF, MY DEAR MONICA!

YOU SAID THAT THIS JUNIOR DANIEL WAS HONEST AND DETER-MINED.
SO, HE CAN'T BE A BAD GUY!
ARGH! YOUR LECTURES ARE TOO TRANSCENDENTAL FOR ME!
YOU THINK MR. LICURGO TAUGHT NICK CRAZY TALKING POINTS?

HE COULD ONLY BE INNOCENT! OR AN IDIOT!
HE IS BEING USED BY ART&TECH.

WHEN HE KNOWS THE TRUTH, HE'LL HELP ME.
I JUST NEED A PLAN!
RIGHT! AND HOW DO YOU EXPECT TO COME UP WITH ONE?

WITH YOUR HELP!

YOU WORRY ABOUT ME, DON'T YOU?

OH, BOY. I CAN'T EVEN DISAGREE...

AN INFALLIBLE PLAN?!

SO, I THOUGHT... WHO BETTER THAN YOU TO COME UP WITH A PLAN?
IT'S RIGHT UP YOUR ALLEY, ISN'T IT?

WHAT?! WHY WOULD I HELP?
THE OTHER DAY YOU ALMOST MADE ME SWALLOW MY JACKET.

RIGHT, THEN. THIS IS YOUR CHANCE TO MAKE IT UP TO ME.
THAT'S WHAT YOU THINK!

WELL, I HAVE A BETTER IDEA! I'LL COME UP WITH YOUR PLAN...
...AND **YOU** MAKE IT UP TO ME BY GOING TO THE MOVIES WITH ME, SOUND GOOD?

WHAT?! THAT'S BLACKMAIL! EXTORTION! YOU... YOU...

FINE!
THEN GO ASK SMUDGE FOR A PLAN!
LATER...
NOOO! OKAY! YOU WIN! I'LL GIVE!
SEND ME THE PLAN, LOWLIFE.

LUCKY FOR YOU THAT I HAVE ALL MY OLD PLANS ON MY LAPTOP!
SO, LET'S SEE...
WE CAN USE A VARIANT OF PLAN 74-B TO CAPTURE THE RABBIT!
WHAT?! OH, YOU--

YOU NEVER KNOW WHEN YOU MIGHT NEED THEM...
...LIKE RIGHT NOW, FOR EXAMPLE?

MOVING ON...
FINDING THE ADDRESS OF A CELEBRITY IS EASY.
YOU JUST NEED TO LOOK IN THE PAGES OF THE NATIONAL ASKER MAGAZINE!

BUT THE PAD OF A MOVIE MEGASTAR SHOULD BE HEAVILY GUARDED!
FILLED WITH GUARDS, DOGS, CAMERAS...

SO, LET'S GET TO THE PLAN! **STEP ONE...**
ASK **FRANKLIN** TO INVENT A WAY TO GET THE **BLUEPRINTS** OF THE HOUSE.
EASY AS PIE! I SAW IT IN A **COMIC!**
HE HAS A MANSION JUST LIKE ANTONIO STARCH, THE GOLDEN ARMOR!
STEP TWO...
SET UP A **LOOKOUT POINT** TO CASE THE JOINT FOR A FEW DAYS.
PLAN? WHAT PLAN?
I **ALWAYS** KEEP WATCH ON CELEBRITY HOUSES, BABYCAKES.
FIND ANOTHER **SPY,** OKAY?

STEP THREE...
FIND THE **SECURITY CAMERAS.**
LOOK FOR A BLIND SPOT... OR CREATE ONE.
A PICTURE IN FRONT OF THE CAMERA? THAT DOESN'T WORK IN REAL LIFE!
SO WHAT? THIS IS A COMIC, REMEMBER?

STEP FOUR...
WAIT FOR THE GUARDS TO BE DISTRACTED BEFORE INFILTRATING!
WOW! THAT MIDDLE-AGED MAN IS TRYING TO JUMP THE FENCE.
MUST BE ANOTHER CRAZY FAN!
I AM NOT CRAZY!
STEP FIVE...
TO NEUTRALIZE THE CANINE THREAT, KEEP A SUPPLY OF TREATS.
WHAT? TREATS?!
DOG TREATS, NOT HUMAN TREATS!
STEP SIX...
SEARCH FOR THE SERVICE ENTRANCE IN THE BACK OF THE HOUSE.

OH, YEAH! I ALMOST FORGOT!
IN CASE YOU MISS A CAMERA...

...OR NOT EVERY GUARD IS DISTRACTED...
STOP, YOU MISCREANT FAN!
TRESPASSING ON PRIVATE PROPERTY, REALLY?

...IT'S BEST TO USE A DISGUISE THAT DOESN'T SEEM TOO OBVIOUS.
HEH... WHO HERE ORDERED THE THREE-CHEESE, MEAT-LOVER, WITH EXTRA ANCHOVIES?
GROSS! I HATE ANCHOVIES...
Pizza

I KNOW, I KNOW...

YOU MUST BE THINKING...

ALL THIS WORK WENT INTO J-FIVE'S PLAN.

AND **EVEN MORE** WORK TO PUT IT INTO PRACTICE.

SO, WHY **DIDN'T** NICK NOPE FOLLOW THE PLAN?

WHY DID MONICA GO IN HIS PLACE?

YOU DON'T KNOW ME THAT WELL, DO YOU?

NOC
NOC
NOC
MAY I COME IN?

HMM. I DIDN'T HEAR A "NO."
FUNNY, THE DOOR WAS UNLOCKED.
THEY MUST HAVE LEFT IT UNARMED WHEN THEY WENT TO INTERCEPT MONICA.

LEAPING SNAILS! THIS IS THE **PARLOR ROOM?**
MY WHOLE HOUSE FITS IN HERE!
-BLAH!- WHAT BAD TASTE!
TOO MUCH GOLD IS GAUDY...

ALL THIS TO INFLATE THE EGO OF SOME BUM OF AN ACTOR AND--

WELL... MAYBE NOT **JUST** A BUM OF AN ACTOR.

>ARGH!< AND WHAT'S THIS?
HE WASN'T EVEN **IN** THESE MOVIES!

I'LL ADMIT, THESE STATUES ARE REALLY AWESOME.
THIS KINGZILLA EVEN SMELLS LIKE SMUDGE.

AND IT STILL DROOLS LIKE AN ORNAMENTAL FOUNTAIN...

CHOMP

IT'S ALIVE!
HE'S STUFFED, MOVES, AND SCARY...

I'M IN LOVE!

ROAAAAAAAAAAR!

I'LL NEVER NEED HAIR GEL AGAIN!
REALLY, I WANT ONE OF THESE FOR MYSELF!

COME HERE, CUTIE! GIVE ME A HUG!
DO YOU THINK IT'S BATTERY OPERATED?
I COULD ASK FRANKLIN TO TRY--
HEY! WHERE'S IT GOING?
COULD IT BE AN ANTITHEFT PROTOCOL?
I JUST WANTED TO BORROW IT.

I KNOW! THE ANIMAL IS PROBABLY **REMOTE CONTROLLED!**

...AND DANIEL ROBERTO SHOULD BE DRIVING IT TO SOME PLACE!
FOLLOW IT AND I FIND THE ACTOR!

GEE, HE EVEN HAS A POOL INSIDE THE HOUSE...
...AND THE POOL HAS A **BRIDGE?**

CHOMP

GRRRAA AARRH!

...BUT YOU CAN FACE MY LASER SWORDS, INVADER!

NOOO! DID YOU HAVE TO END ON THE MOST DRAMATIC PART?
WHAT A CLICHÉ! SO PRE-DICTABLE! I HATE IT!
BET THE FANS WANTED MORE ROMANCE TOO.
SORRY, EVERYONE! SEE YOU NEXT TIME!

Charmz chat™

Welcome to MONICA ADVENTURES #4 “Should I Say Yes… to Nick Nope?” from the conspiracy theorists at Charmz, the Papercutz imprint devoted to romantic and fun graphic novels. We have called MONICA comics royalty a lot, but this year is a special one for her and her creator Mauricio de Sousa. Sousa’s hardworking studio that creates more than 100 MONICA comics annually, Mauricio de Sousa Produções, is celebrating 60 years of comicbook success. It all began with Mauricio’s first comics characters, Franklin and his blue dog, Blu. The real breakout star of those comics, however, was Franklin’s friend Jimmy Five, now called J-Five. That is, until Monica made her fateful appearance in 1963 in the pages of J-Five’s comic strip—starting a 50 year-long battle for the spotlight. Congratulations from all of us at Charmz to Mauricio de Sousa Produções (known affectionately as MSP) and here’s to the next 60 successful years!

ANOS
MSP 2019

Papercutz publishes a number of comic superstars who are also celebrating important anniversaries. No, we aren’t talking about the dinosaurs of DINOSAUR EXPLORERS, but classic titans of the comicbook world. In 2015, everyone’s favorite green clayboy, Art Clokey’s GUMBY, celebrated his 60th anniversary since debuting on TV screens in black and white. Papercutz released GUMBY #1 “50 Shades of Clay” to commemorate the clay-creation who can jump into any book (with his pony pal, Pokey, too!). It’s fun (and semi-flexible if you buy the paperback) and filled with art and stories by Art Baltazar, Veronica and Andy Fish, Kyle Baker, Ray Fawkes, Rick Geary, Jolyon Yates, and more! Last year, certain blue creations, about 3 apples high, and who wear funny white hats and battle a crotchety old sorcerer, celebrated their collective 60th anniversary. That’s right! THE SMURFS are 60 years old! Well, Papa Smurf is 546… The Smurfs first appeared as supporting characters in the *Johan and Peewit* comic series by Belgian comics creator Pierre Culliford, better known as Peyo. Papercutz has published 26 volumes of THE SMURFS graphic novels to date as well as other special format books. Our blue friends have a bright future! Also from the Franco-Belgian realm of comics, this year marks ASTERIX’s 60th anniversary. ASTERIX THE GAUL premiered on October 29, 1959 when writer René Goscinny and cartoonist Albert Uderzo introduced the world to a little

A SPECIAL MESSAGE FROM

MAURICIO DE SOUSA

THE CREATOR OF MONICA (AND NICK NOPE!)

Any adventure with Nick Nope involved cannot unfold naturally nor perform as expected. The boy is adamant in keeping his philosophy sharply polished and his peculiar viewpoint razor focused. Nick's contradictions almost topple Monica without any infallible plan involved, or anything. Sure, these pages are fictional. Everything in this story is contrived… however… when faced with so much fiction, fictional things can start seeming like reality… or vice-versa. So, now that we are at the end of this volume—time for the moral of the story and all that—how about we be careful not to fall for fads? Nick Nope was just warning us about that, was he not? If everyone is wearing red, do you need to wear the same color as well? If everyone wants a Golden Armor for themselves, why do you need one too? An individual is an individual. Everyone has the right to make their own choices, independent of others—Nick Nope is an expert at this—without worrying what others may think. To close… Nick Nope is somebody that we would all like to be sometimes, isn't he?

Until next time.

Mauricio

spitfire who held off an entire Roman invasion of his village thanks to a secret strength potion and then traveled the world. We are proud to announce that we will be publishing ASTERIX in North America with all-new translations of the classic comics, starting in 2020!

Papercutz's legacy of publishing icons of comic history remains as strong as Monica and Asterix themselves. Be it blue Smurfs, or green Gumbys, our comics will be enjoyable for years to come. As for Monica, she will return in MONICA ADVENTURES #5 "Is Nick Nope Right About this One Thing?" Find out wherever fine books are sold!

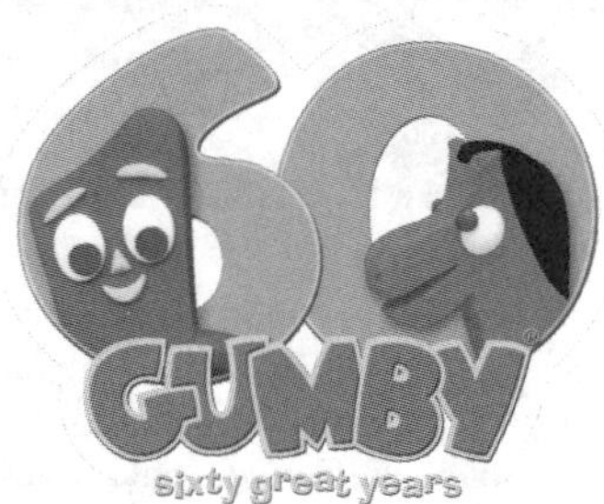

STAY IN TOUCH!

EMAIL:	whitman@papercutz.com
WEB:	Papercutz.com
TWITTER:	@papercutzgn
INSTAGRAM:	@papercutzgn
FACEBOOK:	PAPERCUTZGRAPHICNOVELS
FANMAIL:	Charmz, 160 Broadway, Suite 700, East Wing, New York, NY 10038

MORE GRAPHIC NOVELS AVAILABLE FROM Charmz

STITCHED #1
"THE FIRST DAY OF THE REST OF HER LIFE"

STITCHED #2
"LOVE IN THE TIME OF ASSUMPTION"

G.F.F.s #1
"MY HEART LIES IN THE 90s"

G.F.F.s #2
"WITCHES GET THINGS DONE"

ANA AND THE COSMIC RACE #1
"THE RACE BEGINS"

CHLOE #1
"THE NEW GIRL"

CHLOE #2 "THE QUEEN OF HIGH SCHOOL"

CHLOE #3
"FRENEMIES"

CHLOE #4
"RAINY DAY"

COMING SOON:
CHLOE #5
"CARNIVAL PARTY"

COMING SOON:
CHLOE & CARTOON

SCARLET ROSE #1

SCARLET ROSE #2

SCARLET ROSE #3

SCARLET ROSE #4

MONICA ADVENTURES #1

MONICA ADVENTURES #2

MONICA ADVENTURES #3

MONICA ADVENTURES #4

COMING SOON:
MONICA ADVENTURES #5

AMY'S DIARY #1

AMY'S DIARY #2

AMY'S DIARY #3

SWEETIES #1

SWEETIES #2

SEE MORE AT PAPERCUTZ.COM

NOOOOOOOPE...
You got it all backwards! You can't
read this comic if you start from here.
I understand that the original Japanese
manga is read in the traditional "right to
left" style... But I had a little conversation
with Mauricio and he let us keep our stories
the way we are accustomed to - from left
to right. Let's agree that even though these
comics have a manga style that we respect
very much, there is still much of the
original Monica's Gang in them too...
Enjoy!
Monica.
"IT ALL STARTED TODAY AFTER CLASS..."
HA-HA! HA-HA!
AW "J", YOU ARE SO ADORABLE!
WHAT?
GULP! UM... I SAID "THAT LAST ONE WAS HORRIBLE"!
REALLY?!
GOOD THINGS OR BAD?
ALRIGHTY!